THE GR   :K

and other stories

*Earlier short stories published
on behalf of the author*

Messages (2011)
Never Was There Tale of Brighter Hue (2013)
The Grey Lady (2015)
The Butterfly Effect (2020)

THE
GRANDFATHER
CLOCK

AND OTHER STORIES

Peter Dawson

Published by Peter Dawson
30 Elm Street
Borrowash
Derby, DE72 3HP

British Library Cataloguing-in-Publication data
A catalogue record for this book is available from the British
Library

ISBN 978-1-8383404-2-1

Typeset by Carnegie Book Production, Lancaster
Printed and bound by Jellyfish Solutions Ltd

CONTENTS

ABOUT THE AUTHOR

Peter Dawson, a graduate of the LSE, was from 1970, for ten years, the headmaster of an Inner London mixed comprehensive school for two thousand pupils. In 1980 he became the first General Secretary of the Professional Association of Teachers, one of the six teachers' unions at that time. After twelve combative years of that, he moved on to lead a team of Ofsted school inspectors. He was sent as a UK delegate to the economic and social assembly of the European Community in Brussels, which was no less combative than education politics had been. He was appointed an OBE. He subsequently served for twelve years as a lay member of the Employment Appeal Tribunal in London, hearing appeals against the decisions of local employment tribunals. A regular newspaper columnist and broadcaster in his heyday, he is now an ordained Minister of the Methodist Church. Happily and securely married for over sixty years, a father and a grandfather, he is a sponsor of the Family Education Trust, which promotes traditional family values.

Talent alone cannot make a writer.
There must be a life behind the book.

Johann Goethe

THE
GRANDFATHER CLOCK

Augustus Filbert was a sixty-seven year old bachelor whose successful career in merchant banking had brought him great wealth. His suits were made in Savile Row and his shoes were made to order by one of London's most eminent shoemakers. His butler ensured that he never left his house looking anything less than immaculate.

Some said that Augustus, with his perfectly trimmed moustache, was the equal in his careful presentation of himself of the fictional detective Hercule Poirot. He knew some of his friends said so and, being of inquisitive disposition, he decided one evening to watch one of the stories about Agatha Christie's famous sleuth on television. In Poirot, he saw a man after his own heart in his fastidious appearance and in his desire to see everything in its place on his desk and elsewhere in his living space. Augustus decided that did not mind in the least being compared with Poirot. Without saying so to anyone, he felt the comparison was entirely justified.

Augustus lived in a detached house built to his design overlooking the Sussex downs. His interest was in beautiful furniture and in oil paintings. His acquisitions in those fields were carefully displayed in his house, where he occasionally held dinner parties for his neighbours so that they might look upon his treasures. He had the most highly sophisticated alarm system against burglary that had ever been invented.

Hearing that Christie's were going to auction three of Winston Churchill's oil paintings, he eagerly prepared to attend. He booked a room at the Dorchester and travelled up to London first class by train. He liked using the train because the countryside between Sussex and the London outskirts was so beautiful. But he became irritable when the train entered the London suburbs, with daubing on all the walls beside the railway. He called the approach to London graffiti land.

He arrived at Christie's well before the auction in order to view the items for sale. Staff were in attendance to answer questions, and to provide security. Augustus had been at a Christie's auction before and was once told, 'We get some very funny people here, nosing round before an auction, but our staff are experienced in dealing with them. The police respond quickly to any calls we make.'

Augustus examined Churchill's oil paintings and fell for a French coastal scene. The great man painted many of that kind, often having been seen sitting in the sun in front of his easel, cigar in his mouth, overlooking some small French harbour. He was serious about his painting and had once declared that, when he was dead, he intended to spend his first thousand years in eternity getting to the bottom of this business of painting in oils. Some said he wasn't making a bad job of it this side of the hereafter.

Suddenly, he who came intending to bid for a Churchill painting found his attention drawn to a magnificent grandfather clock. He moved closer to examine it. The housing was of beautiful English oak which shone in a beam of early morning sunlight entering the room from a nearby window. The Roman numerals on the clock face were delicately inlaid in black ebony. The clock was clearly of great age but superbly preserved. Augustus felt an attendant move close to him. 'It's a beauty, isn't it?' said the attendant quietly, 'Would you like to know more about it?'

The clock, breathtaking in its own right, also had an interesting history. Built in 1815 by the distinguished clockmakers Packfield & Prince Limited, it was made in response to an order from the Earl of Liverpool. The Earl was Prime Minister at the time and wanted to celebrate England's victory at Waterloo. He said, 'Napoleon's time is up and this clock will say so.'

'The earl was insistent that the clock should be made of fine English oak as a monument to England's victory', said the attendant. He explained that it was made at a time when a particular species of ebony was used in mosaic work and in providing decorative inlays in furniture of the highest grade. The attendant said, 'The use of ebony on the dial of a clock was, according to our research, unique. We believe the Earl of Liverpool wanted the grandfather clock to be superior to any of the kind ever made before.'

'It's interesting', said the attendant, 'to think that this clock ticked away to mark victory over England's enemies at Waterloo and was still ticking away to mark Churchill's similar triumph.' Augustus thought to himself that the attendant knew his business as a salesman. He inquired, 'What are Christie's expecting the clock to go for in the auction?' 'Well', came the response, 'a piece in *The Times* said we are expecting six figures. I can't see it going for less than a hundred thousand, and it might reach two.'

The man paused, then added, 'Excuse me, sir, but am I right in thinking you are the gentleman who bought the Queen Anne solid silver candelabra a your ago?' 'Yes', replied Augustus, 'and my guests were greatly impressed when it stood in the centre of the table at dinner. Candles enhanced the beauty of the silver. which shone to great effect. Just wait till my friends see this magnificent clock. I must have it.'

Augustus asked the attendant if there was a telephone he could use to ring his broker. Guessing the inquirer's intention, the attendant conducted Augustus to a telephone in an adjacent room. When he got through, Augustus identified himself and asked to speak urgently to Charles Grant, the most senior figure at Grant and Sons Stockbrokers. His request brought an immediate response.

'Good morning, Augustus', came the businesslike but cheery greeting. 'Good morning Charles', came the response, 'I'm at Christies's and need to put a few hundred thousand into my bank account.' Charles laughed, 'Now what is it you are after? Another treasure to add to your collection?'

'That's right', responded Augustus, 'I'd like you to sell all my Treasury bonds and transfer the money into my bank account without delay. The interest rate on the bonds is not up to much.' Charles Grant, impressed with his caller's financial acumen, said, 'We'll sell the bonds today and I hope you get what you are after.' 'Oh, I will, I will', came the confident reply. Charles had not doubt it would happen. He had never known Augustus Filbert to fail to acquire whatever he was after.

Augustus left Christie's a happy man at midday, having acquired both a Churchill painting and the grandfather clock. He had spent a considerable amount of money but both objects he had bought were rock solid securities for the future.

He lunched at the Carlton Club, where he was a member, then went to Jermyn Street to buy some cigars to celebrate. He strolled through St James' Park in the sunshine and went to Charing Cross to buy *The Economist* in the station. He was amused to hear the music coming over the tannoy: Abba singing Waterloo. He had an afternoon sleep in his room at the Dorchester and, after dinner in the evening, watched *An Inspector Calls* on television. He was glad he had no wife or family to disturb his peace of mind.

Sitting on the train home after staying overnight at the Dorchester, Augustus found himself planning a dinner party at which he would be able to show people his latest treasures. Just short of a year after that event, Augustus died suddenly of a heart attack. In an addendum to his will, he had bequeathed the grandfather clock to the Carlton Club, to which political leaders often belonged, and those aspiring to govern the nation.

There was a great debate at the club as to the clock's location. From the reception area, a wide staircase led up to a large landing from which a further staircase to the left led to the dining room and another to the right to the lounge. It was decided that the landing was the ideal place for the clock. There it sat, looking down on dignitaries and men of power in politics and business as they mounted the stairs. As for the clock, having found a new home, it just went on ticking like before as it watched more history being made.

Not long after it had been put in place, a group of club members stood at the foot of the stairs, looking up at the clock and admiring it. One said, 'Do you remember the song we used to sing in school about a grandfather clock that stopped ticking when the old man who owned it died?' 'Oh yes', said one, excited at the memory. There was muted, kindly laughter as someone else said, 'But now it's our friend Augustus who has stopped short, never to go again.'

DECISIONS FOR LIFE

'What', demanded Miss Bullivant, 'will your father say?' Miss B, as she was known in the school, where she had been on the staff for over twenty years, was teaching her lower sixth A Level English group. They were studying Priestley's *An Inspector Calls*, which has to do, *inter alia*, with the decisions people make in life and the disasters to which the wrong ones may lead.

'All of you', she said, looking round the twelve girls in the group, 'have some big decisions to make this school year. Are you heading for university? If yes, what do you want to study? Choose carefully with a view to whatever future you have in mind. Carol, how about you?' 'I want to go to Durham and read English, then get a PGCE and teach in a school like this', the girl replied.

'Excellent', said Miss B to her best A Level candidate, a girl whose academic ability was matched by what had always been a thoroughly conformist attitude to the multitude of rules and expectations governing life in this highly traditional school.

Molly Sugden's hand went up and the teacher

pursed her lips. The girl had often shown a tendency to challenge authority. She also seemed to Miss B to have far too much interest in the boys at the school next door. 'Right Molly', she said, 'what is your ambition?' 'Please miss', she replied, 'I want to marry a good-looking man with lots of money and have six children.' The other girls laughed and one of them said, 'She will, too. It will be nappies all the way.'

Miss B sighed and turned her attention to Penny Radford, a much more palatable prospect. She was regarded by the science staff as the best student they had ever had. 'Tell us Penny', she said, smiling, 'what are you going to do after your first degree? Stay on for a masters, then do research for a PhD? I can see you making a career in the academic world.'

Penny groaned inside. She was a modest, unassuming girl who took her academic ability for granted, having once responded to a request from another sixth former who was struggling with physics to explain why she found it easy by replying, 'I don't know. God gave me my brains, not Father Christmas.' She laughed and added, 'He also made me hopeless at hockey.'

Penny knew that Miss B would not like the answer to what her teacher had asked, but she decided to be clear about what she intended. She said, 'I'm not going to university. I'm applying for a place at nursing school. I want a career with my sleeves rolled up, caring for the sick. I'm really a practical person.'

'It's true', said Molly, 'she mended my bike when the chain broke.' Others laughed and nodded their heads. 'Miss', said one of them, 'when we had the children from the school for the disabled, Penny knew how to handle them right away. They ended up hanging on to her and not wanting to leave. She's got some magic inside.'

Miss B was not impressed. Fixing her attention on Penny, she said, 'But what will your father say?' James Radford was Chief Education Officer at the offices of the local education authority. Miss B was sure he would not hear of what his daughter intended. Otherwise, she thought, he was not fit to have such a clever daughter. Miss B was about to discover that her understanding of men, a species she had avoided all her life, was limited. She found them intimidating.

'My father', said Penny, 'thinks I will make a good nurse. He says he's glad he helped to produce a daughter who will be trained to look after him in his old age. My dad's a bit of a comedian, you see. But he also said that my future is for me to decide. He says he trusts me and will support me whatever I decide to do.' She paused and added, 'He's wonderful.'

Jackie Benson, sitting behind Penny, wished she had a father like that. When she told hers that her dream was to enter farming and work with animals he had said, 'No way. You're not doing that. You were born for something better than being a bloody milk maid. Anyway, I need you in my business.' When she protested that she wanted to go to college and study modern animal husbandry, he flew into a rage. He was a solicitor and Jackie could think of nothing worse than being at a desk sorting out people's legal problems, especially if it meant working under her father, whom she regarded as a male chauvinist pig.

Jackie leaned forward to Penny and said, 'You don't know how lucky you are. I will have to run away from home to do what I want to do.' Then she thought a bit and said, 'But I think my lovely mum will help me pack.' She laughed and added. 'She might even come with me!'

Miss B was still unhappy with Penny when she got back to the staff room. 'These girls today', she said to a group of young colleagues appointed in recent years, 'seem to have no respect for their parents. They think they can go their own way regardless. But it's hardly surprising when you discover how some parents encourage them to make their own decisions. I think that may lead to disaster. See if I'm not right if that fine girl Penny Radford ends up simply emptying bed pans.'

Mary Woolmer, twenty-two, new to the staff and recently married, said *sotto voice* to a nearby colleague, 'It's Miss B who's the disaster. She knows nothing of the way things are changing. The girls in this school are going to remake the world.' Thoughtfully, she went on, 'But my man worries about boys. He thinks they will be left wondering about their place in society. I tell him not to be concerned because I will always find him something to do. I remind him about putting the bins out as I say that.' Miss B overheard this and said, 'That's all men are good for in my humble opinion; and making babies for the education system.'

That opinion was interestingly explored at the next school prizegiving. The speaker was a young woman who was a powerful figure in the newspaper industry. She felt the invitation to speak at the school was an opportunity not to be missed. She smiled mischievously as she fearlessly declaimed, 'Girls, the world is changing. You are destined to overcome years of women being subject to the dictates of men. Yours is the generation in which women will take power. The day will come when young men will wonder about their role.' She laughed as she added, 'But I guess we'll still need them to help maintain the population.' Mary Woolmer felt warm inside as she said to herself, 'That's what him and me are about to do.'

The speaker had released an embargoed copy of her speech to the media and the coverage next day was moderately sensational. The girls in Miss B's A

Level English group were excited by it, especially Jackie Benson, whose determination to study animal husbandry became absolute, even if she had to run away.

A WAITING GAME

'Life', said the lecturer, 'is a waiting game. As children, we wait impatiently to grow up. In adolescence, we wait for our hormones to stop messing us about; for the right boy or girl to come along. We wait nervously for offers of university places and, even more nervously, for our A Level results. We wait for an opportunity to leave home and take on the world; to discover who we really are.'

John Register, lecturer in the elements of social stucture in the sociology department at Liverpool Aintree University, paused. 'And that', he said, launching himself into a further catalogue of life's challenges, 'is only the start. After you graduate, you will wait to be admitted to whatever employment you choose to realise the future you have in mind. You may also still be waiting for the right boy or girl to come along. Solve that problem and you will soon be waiting to buy a house and waiting to start a family.'

John Register paused again and said, 'And so on and so on and so on. Life is a waiting game. But there's a Zen saying: *Nothing happens next. This is it.* Rather than wait for the next turn of events; for the next moment of decision; for the next unfolding of the future, concentrate on where you are now and make the most of it.'

'That's pretty good advice as you launch yourselves into your studies here. Forget about what might come next. It's what you do in the next three years that matters. For you, now, this is it. There's a message emblazoned on the wall of the dining room of a sixth form college near here. It says: *Don't wait to start work. The moment to start is now.*'

The hundreds of freshers in front of the lecturer, who traditionally delivered a welcome to the new intake at the university, were attending closely to what was being said. Many of them were taking notes. John Register smiled to himself on seeing this, remembering a rather cynical observation by a colleague. Harry Bixby, a senior lecturer specializing in the history of social mobility, insisted that by the time students get to their final year, they don't make many notes. 'They take careful notes in their second year, but freshers scribble down everything you say.' He asserted, 'If you start your first lecture by saying good morning, they write it down.'

A student named Jake Fordham was very unhappy at what John Register had said about getting down to work straight away. He had understood that the first weeks at university were devoted to freshers' boozy parties and casual sex. He had already spotted a girl to whom he would like to give the pleasure of his attention.

The first departmental meeting of sociology staff at the start of a new academic year was always aleatory. What came up was a matter of chance, depending on whether or not someone had come back from the vacation with an axe to grind. Professor Bernard Woakes was likely to be chief axe-grinder.

After twenty years of promoting social theory in face of those encouraging social action, Woakes had become quite irritable. He regarded the rise of activist protest as threatening the social fabric upon which the British way of life was built. The world of social theory was his safe haven but fewer students than was once the case were interested in the analysis of tradition and its purposes. Woakes sometimes used his position as chairman of departmental meetings to obstruct the agents of revolution, namely the young lecturers who encouraged students who wanted to change the world and had come up to read sociology with that purpose.

Calling the meeting to order, Woakes began by introducing a new member of staff. Saffi Omolo had been appointed to introduce a new element to the curriculum, namely Social Equality. She had been not the Professor's choice. He had been excluded from the selection process. The Vice-Chancellor believed, and his senior colleagues agreed, that the sociology department was behind the times.

Launching the department gathering, Woakes said, 'We welcome Miss Saffi Omolo to the staff.' He got no further. Smiling, the newcomer interjected. 'I am not Miss Saffi Omolo.' She spat out the word Miss as if she had had a putrid fish stuffed down her throat. 'Perhaps I'm married, perhaps not. Whatever, I don't agree with prefixing women's names to clarify whether or not they are legally tied to a man. Why should women have to put up with that? Just call me Saffi.' The two women on the staff of fifteen looked at one another. 'We have been waiting for this', whispered one to the other. Harold Jacobs, a young lecturer who yearned for someone to shake up the department, told himself the new academic year was going to be exciting.

And so it proved. Saffi's first lecture was a sensation. Addressing the students who had chosen the Social Equality course, she opened up with, 'Did they warn you that I am seriously disabled? Oh, yes I am. I'm a woman and I am black. Not coloured. As black as Newgate's knocker. That's a description of the knocker on the door of Newgate Prison they used in the old days to emphasise blackness.' She went on: 'As if being a black woman is not a sufficient disability, I am also slow over a hundred metres. You can amount to something as a black woman athlete today, but that's about it.'

She paused to gather her breath before delivering her punch line: 'The only black woman who achieved fame in the high days of the old film industry played Mammy in 'Gone With the Wind', and her part was that of a slave.'

'Social equality? Just being a woman, never mind about your colour, is still a handicap today. As of now, there are sixteen staff in the sociology department of this university, but only three of them are women and only one of them is not white.'

'But inequality is not just a problem for women or for blacks and those labelled ethnic minorities by the Islington intelligentsia. Some young white men have many handicaps. Those stuck in the bottom streams at school don't have much of a future because our education system is fixated on academic ability. Those from homes where parents have no interest in them soon lose interest in getting anywhere. And now that women want to be free of the old constraints of married life and dependence on men, boys growing up today struggle to understand their role in society.'

'I'm delighted'. said Saffi, 'If some of you think I'm talking a load of nonsense, or if I've confused you. It means we're going to have a great time arguing with one another this academic year. Perhaps it will change some of your thinking. I guess it will change some of mine. Let's all wait and see. Life, you know, is sometimes a waiting game.'

'Wow', said Jake Fordham as he left the lecture, 'I've never fancied a black woman before but this one is the goods.' Others had been captivated by Saffi's exposition. That was hardly surprising because the group had a couple of hours earlier attended Bernard Woakes' introductory lecture. He had chosen as his subject the philosophical basis of the social structure in ancient Greece. It had reminded one student of a novel in which a teacher of Greek at a public school had been nicknamed 'Ditchy'. He told a young woman he was walking out with, 'It means ditchwater. Dull as.'

Hearing about Saffi's opening lecture as it was discussed excitedly by some of the staff who had chosen to attend, Bernard Woakes was appalled. 'What have we done?' he expostulated to a colleague who had been at the university as long as he had and who shared his opposition to change. But within five years, Bernard and the old guard had gone and the teaching of sociology had been transformed.

But Saffi had gone too. After six years as an MP she had become a junior minister and two years after that was sitting on the front bench of the Labour Opposition in the House of Commons. Her political career had taken off like a rocket. Her maiden speech had caused an uproar in the House and in the media. In an education debate about standards in schools, it was reported that the poor performance of boys of black ethnic origin was a serious problem.

Sir Basil Brace-Atkins, MP for Buckingham and a Tory of the old stripe, rose to assert that blacks were known to be of limited intellect and to be constitutionally indolent. Saffi got to her feet from the backbenches and was called by the Speaker. Drawing in her breath, she declaimed: 'The trouble with people like the Member for Buckingham is that he still thinks we blacks are the white man's burden. Well let me tell him that, in the world of today, men like him are the black man's burden. And he's a bigger burden than my ancestors in Africa ever were.' There were roars of approval on the Labour benches. The Speaker interjected. 'Personal insults', he said, 'are not permitted in this House. I will not say more than that to the Member for Lewisham as she is a newcomer.' He paused, smiled and added, 'Please unburden yourself with greater care.'

This Saffi proceeded to do, but with no diminution in her effect. Spelling out the handicaps under which black people laboured, as she had done in her Social Equality lectures and seminars, she covered with fluency what was required for ethnic minorities to succeed in schools. 'Ask yourselves', she said, 'why young people from China do so well. You did know about that, didn't you? Get your minds round that.' She felt ready to answer her own question but realized it might be a problem for the Shadow Minister for Education so she quietly subsided with the eyes of many MPs upon her.

Her opening salvo hit the media headlines and the *Guardian* arranged an interview. A member of the sociology department at the university said, 'I see our Saffi has erupted in Parliament already. Watch this space.' Two of Saffi's closest colleagues and supporters in the department, learning that she was trying for a seat in Parliament, had advised her to be in less of a hurry to leave behind her success in the university world. In response, she had said: 'I know life is sometimes a matter of waiting, but I just can't wait to get into the political jungle and change society for the better. Zen teaching says nothing happens next. But it does. For me, the next thing has arrived. This is it.'

RABBITS

Once upon a time there lived on a certain hillside a colony of rabbits. They had elected one of their number, Bigbun, to rule over them. He was a descendent of the most famous rabbit in history, Bunoses, of whom more later. Bigbun was very large, spoke with authority, and was good at sorting out bunnious disputes. Despite his size, he was very kindly and widely regarded as bunevolent.

Most of the colony lived in burrows but a few, who were of an architectural disposition, erected superior accommodation above ground made of branches knitted together and sealed with mud. They were very cosy and let in the light and were known as bungalows. There were about twenty of them scattered across the hillside and they were the envy of those whose lived underground in the burrows. 'Them up there are better off than us. It's not fair', said a young rabbit with radical tendencies, 'I'd like to start a bunolution.' Bunnymum said, 'Don't be silly. Rabbits are made to be stroked, not to fight.'

In school, the most important subject taught to the young was bunistory. Each generation learned how the colony had come to occupy the pleasant hillside they called home. Years before, the original members had live happily together on a hill far away but it had been invaded by a tribe of foxes who drove them out. Their journey to find another hill was long and tiring.

The bunexodus from their old home to a new one was known in bunistory as the Great Buntrek. They had all kinds of adventures in their search for a new home, and young bunnies had to learn them all. The most challenging tale was when the Great Buntrek came to a wide stream.

Rabbits can't swim. Seeing the water, some of them said to Bunoses, the leader, 'Why did you bring us here to drown attempting to cross. We should have stayed at the old place and negotiated with the foxes.' 'Yes', said others, 'our feet are aching and some of us have developed bunions.' Bunoses just smiled and said, 'Have faith ...'

Some became impatient to move on but as the sun shone the lazy days were idyllic. The youngest bunnies loved gambolling in the meadow beside the stream. The rest lay under the shade of nearby trees, listening to rabbit raconteurs telling outrageous tales of when rabbits ruled the earth and grew golden fur.

As the summer sunshine became ever more heated, the water from the nearby hillside that fed the stream became less and less. In due course, rocks and large pebbles began to appear above the water. 'Come' announced Bunoses one morning, 'the lazy days are over. We can cross the stream by hopping over the stones.' The youngest rabbits thought that was great fun while the rest were a little bit sad at leaving their leisurely way of life in the sunshine. And so it came about that the Great Buntrek crossed the bed of the stream and moved on to a new hillside home.

As in all telling of history, events become elaborated and reinterpreted, and this was the case in bunistory. After a time, only a few of those who had taken part in the Great Buntrek were still alive and their memories were dim. So it came about that accounts of the crossing of the stream developed a new dimension. Later generations were taught that the waters had parted when Benoses had prayed to Bungod for help, at which point a path through the waters of the stream opened up, which is to say there was a miracle. Some cynical rabbits who did not believe in Bungod said, 'What a load of bunkum.'

As in most societies, the young became restless as they grew up. At that stage they were called bunteens and could be a real worry to their parents, especially if they wished to leave the colony to see the world. This was called wanting to bunk off.

One day, a bunteen said to his father, 'Father, I'm fed up with rabbit life on a hillside. I would like to go and explore life in the town that lies a few miles from here. The sounds we can hear coming from there sound so exciting. Will you let me bunk off and explore the town?' On hearing this, his parents were sad but they were wise and said, 'We understand that you are growing up and want to spread your floppy ears. But promise us you will come back if you don't take to town life.'

Bernard, for that was the bunteen's name, set off with a song in his heart and sang it to himself on the way. He recited to himself a favourite poem learned at school. It was by Thomas Graybun in 'An Anthology of Bunnitry' and was about a rabbit exploring a churchyard:

A rabbit likes to find a place,
As a member of the bunny race,
To hop around for fun
Like every other bun.
A churchyard's just the place
Where a rabbit may be safe
Until the sunset's glow
Tells him homeward he must go

As he skipped along, Bernard looked forward to finding a place where he'd not been before. He knew there would be lots of hoomins there.

Miss Bunworthy had taught all the young rabbits about hoomins in school. There were so many of them in a town that it was difficult for a rabbit not to get trodden on. Even more dangerous were the machines that puffed out smelly smoke.

Bernard found a cosy spot in the corner of a park and enjoyed himself watching little hoomins on a swing. He thought he would wait until nightfall to look round. He knew life in the town got exciting after dark. Fortunately, he had brought a piece of turnip to eat so he wasn't hungry. But when the night time came, he felt rather cold and, when he went exploring the town, was very, very disappointed.

What had sounded from a distance to be music and laughter turned out to be just a noisy twanging sound and hammering of drums, with laughter coming from a place where adult hoomins seemed to have lost control of themselves. He had heard all about that sort of thing in his health education lessons at school. He remembered his teacher, Miss Bunworthy, saying how silly hoomins were when it came to food and drink. She said, 'They eat too much and grow fat, then they drink too much and act crazy. They go absolutely bunanas.'

All the class realised that going bunanas was an extremely dreadful thing, though they were not sure what made hoomins go that way from lapping up water. Jimmy Bunstone, a boy who often misbehaved in class, went out after the lesson and lapped up some water in a puddle in the playground, then danced about like crazy.

'Stop that', said Miss Bunworthy, standing at the school door. Everyone froze, including Jimmy. The teacher said, 'It's alright children. Jimmy is only pretending. But going crazy from drinking is not something to joke about. It gets hoomins in all kinds of trouble.'

After his disappointing exploration of the town, Bernard went back to the park and curled up to sleep. Next morning he headed home. He was ever so pleased to see that his father was waiting to welcome him. His father was relieved to see him. He called all the rabbits together to clap Bernard home. He thought he might have lost his bunteen but was ever so glad he had found his way home. 'He might have ended up dead', he said, 'but he's as alive as ever.'

'So', said Bernard's father, 'what have you learned?' Bernard, who was quite buntelligent, replied, 'That what may seem inviting at a distance can be a great disappointment; and that the place for a rabbit is with other rabbits.' 'Well done', said his father, 'your bunking off has been very worthwhile. We'll have a party tonight to celebrate your return. We'll have your favourite – bunny lettice masala.' 'Yum. Yum' said Bernard, 'it's good to be home.'

LOVE BIRDS

'Hullo you two love birds'. Jake and Susie were walking down the road, hand in hand, past Mrs Blakey. Jake was walking Susie home after they had spent Saturday morning together. Mrs B was standing at her open front door in here wrap around apron, having jut scrubbed her door step. 'Hullo Mrs B', replied the young couple, smiling.

Mrs B was a local institution. Everybody knew her and she knew everybody, and their business. If you wanted to know what was going on in the locality, she was the one to ask. Some called her the news of the world. But she was not a gossip and had a heart of gold. If any of her neighbours was in trouble, she would be the first to offer help, despite having a husband and two children to look after herself. Most working class communities had several Mrs Bs. It was how folk survived.

'You know', said Jake to the girl whose hand he clutched so firmly in his own, 'I ought to do a piece on Mrs B. The woman living three doors down from her, Mrs Lockyer, reckons she and her family would not have managed when her hubby lost his caretaking job but for Mrs B. Mr Lockyer is in work again now so Mrs B is on the lookout for someone else to help. I'm sure the editor would be interested. I'll ask her about it tomorrow. I'm fed up with just doing the weekly court report on the misdeeds of local villains.'

Jake was a reporter on the local rag. It was his first job on leaving school three years before when he was seventeen. He had stayed on at school into the lower sixth but left after a year. He was impatient to get on with a writing career. He wanted to publish his first novel by the time he was twenty-five as a preliminary to fame. He had flourished at school as a writer, with many pieces in the school magazine, including his poetry, but had never found possible to get down to work in maths or science.

Summing up his performance at school, his final report said: 'Jake is outstanding in his use of words, which is where his future must surely lie, but the world of numbers remains a mystery to him.' The author of those words smiled at his assessment of Jake's strengths and weaknesses. He thought the carefully balanced sentence was rather clever. He was a schoolmaster of the old-fashioned kind, unaffected by modern thinking on never being discouraging, even at the cost of stating the bald truth. He had once simply written on the report of a boy in the lower school who was a persistent truant, 'Who?'

Jake had not been offended by his final report but smiled at its accuracy. On leaving school, he got a job on the *Bramley Mercury* by making a nuisance of himself with the Polly Richmond, the editor. He had called at the offices of the newspaper with samples of his work from the school magazine, and other stuff he had written. The deputy editor hadn't even looked at Jake's work. 'We have all the reporters we need', was the verdict.

There was a crash in the centre of Bramley between a bus and two cars driven by young lunatics racing one another down the busy high street. Jake wrote a vivid and arresting piece about it, addressed it to Polly Richmond at the *Bramley Mercury,* enclosed a note of his address and telephone number, marked the envelope PRIVATE AND CONFIDENTIAL and posted it.

Polly invited the audacious young man for an interview, there being no doubt that he knew how to write. She was in her thirties, rather casually dressed but clearly a woman of today. She had a reputation for making mincemeat of any of the male chauvinist species who crossed her path. There were many such in the journalistic profession.

'Well', she said to Jake, who was seated before her, 'what makes you want to write for my newspaper. Journalism at this level can be pretty dull, you know. Suppose I sent you to report on cases at the local magistrates court. You'd get bored.' Jake decided to boldly go where maybe none of Polly's reporters might have gone before. He said, 'A good reporter can make anything interesting. The level of minor crime in Bramley deserves to be reported in a dramatic way.' 'OK', said Polly, 'you can have a job for two days a week as our court reporter.'

'It's not much, but it's a start', Jake told them at home. He supplemented his meagre wages by writing a monthly story for *Woman's Own* and by producing book reviews for *The Times Literary Supplement.* The second of those activities convinced him that some writers were unable to write as well as he did himself. 'You're like Bernard Levin', said Jake's contact at the litsupp, 'your reviews are more interesting than the books you write about.'

Then Jake met and fell in love with Susie. She worked in the box office at the Bramley Theatre, where a repertory company produced a different play each week. When they did *A Midsummer Night's Dream*, he was keen to see it because he had studied it at school and played Bottom the weaver in the school production when he was in the lower sixth.

When Jake went to the theatre to buy a ticket, there were few left. But the girl in the box office was very helpful, showing him where the remaining seats were located and indicating which of them was the best. When he went to pay, he found he had left his wallet at home. He apologized profusely but the girl said, 'That's alright. I'll put your ticket aside for you. You look like an honest sort of chap.' She gave him a radiant smile. He was, as they say, captivated.

The production of Shakespeare's famous comedy was a triumph. Jake submitted a piece about it which appeared in the *Bramley Mercury*. He decided to go and see the next play to be performed. On the front of the box office, there was his account of *The Midsummer Night's Dream* on display. 'Hullo again', said the captivating girl in the box office, 'do you see that our last production got a great write-up in the paper. Have you read it?' Jake saw his opportunity. He took a deep breath and said, 'Yes, I wrote it and please will you come out with me?'

As the love story developing between Jake and Susie unfolded, he realized the need also to develop his career. Happily, events made that possible. One day, when he was at the local newspaper office, he had a telephone call from the *Daily Express*. Would he be interested in a job with them? One of the editorial team had seen some of his stuff and had suggested to the editor that Jake might be worth chatting up. Three weeks later, Jake was writing for the *Daily Express*. A month after that, he and Susie had found a flat in London and were making wedding plans.

On returning from their honeymoon, the couple travelled down from London to Bramley to visit

Susie's old home and see her widowed mother. Hand in hand, they passed Mrs Blakey standing at her open front door. 'Hullo you two love birds,' she called out. In her news of the world role, she added, 'Susie, your mum tells me you two have got married.' She paused and smilingly added, 'I knew you would.' 'Hullo Mrs B', the couple replied, 'So did we.'

HAIKU OF THE SEASONS

Haiku is a Japanese form of word play.
It does not lend itself easily to English
but it is fun to try. The metric format is
7.5.7 There are no rhymes or punctuation.

When it is a summer's day
Sunshine embraces
Smiles are on most faces then

When it is a winter's day
Children laugh in snow
Old folk cold much misery

Welcome spring and autumn days
Senses respond first
To fresh then golden beauty

REVENGE

Newbury Little Theatre, one of a string of small theatres staging amateur productions in the 1950s, decided to stage *Twelfth Night.* There was great enthusiasm for the theatre in all its forms after the war before television – what one journalist called the idiot's window – came along to make theatregoing a minor activity.

John Bateson, just out of drama school and earning a living as a porter at the local hospital, played Malvolio in the Newbury amateur production of *Twelfth Night.* The local paper said his great exit line was delivered with frightening power. Dirty and dishevelled, he turned upon his tormenters, who had made a fool of him, then swung round to include the audience, who had laughed at him, in his malevolent glare. In a voice full of menace, he declared, 'I'll be revenged on the whole pack of you.'

Shakespeare had never written a sequel so Malvolio's revengeful intention was never realized on stage. But the day came when the actor who played him at Newbury developed a taste for revenge.

The object of his taste was Alan Ackroyd, with whom he had once had a close relationship at school. The pair had been locked together in the second row of the scrum in the rugby first fifteen. With the hooker and two props in front of them, the five young men had been a powerful unit that opponents feared. Jack Jolson, the hooker, said, 'Them two behind us could push an elephant off a cliff.' It was a *double entendre* because he and the two locks were all doing history at A level and their teacher, a twenty-two stone giant, was nicknamed Heffylump.

As well as rugby and history, John and Alan also had something else in common: both hoped for acting careers, having performed in school productions. On leaving school they ended up at the same drama school. There, their previous close relationship evaporated as their development diverged. Their different personalities became dominant.

Alan was an extrovert, with a driven and vivacious manner and a great sense of humour. John, who had always been quieter, became nervous and withdrawn in face of the demands of drama teachers who struggled to get him to open up and perform. At the end of his first year, he was called in to see the principal who told him did not have what it took to make a career on stage.

Sitting in the bar with others on his last day before leaving, most were sympathetic, but not

Alan. He was full of himself, having just been cast to play Henry Higgins in the drama school's forthcoming production of *Pygmalion*. He said, 'What are you going to do, John? I guess you'll end up as an ASM with special responsibility for props!' Others were unable to stop themselves joining in with Alan's laughter. It was a running joke among drama students that failing to get beyond assistant stage manager was the pits.

Alan's acting career flourished and his name began to appear in the papers. Meanwhile, John became a member of an amateur company and worked as a hospital porter. But he yearned to work on stage as a professional and took a job as an ASM at Maidstone Playhouse, supplementing his meagre income with a part-time job at a local garden centre. He sometimes thought the dahlias had more of a future than him.

He groaned on seeing that a touring production of *Slaughter on Saturday*, a murder thriller, was coming to the Playhouse starring Alan Ackroyd. A preview in the Maidstone Mercury said:

Maidstone Playhouse is lucky to have attracted the Sharkfin Stage Company to its stage. Regulars at playhouse productions will be looking forward to seeing Alan Ackroyd. Before joining Sharkfin, one of our most distinguished touring companies, Alan was nominated for an award for his brilliant performance in *Look Back in Anger* at the Young Vic in London.

John Bateson, ASM with responsibility for props at the theatre where Alan would be performing, wanted to crawl in a hole and hide. If Alan laughed at him when they renewed their acquaintance, there would be a case of Saturday slaughter right there on the stage.

At a critical point in the play, the character Alan was playing, a millionaire who had seduced another man's wife, was shot dead by the cuckolded husband. That was not the end of the play but, as things turned out, it was the end of Alan Ackroyd.

John, in charge of props, was always meticulous in his preparation. He was particularly so when it came to the revolver the husband would use. It had six cylinders to house six bullets. On Monday each week, John would carefully load six blank cartridges, one for each performance from Monday to Saturday, there being no matinees.

On the Monday of Sharkfin's final week at Maidstone, John prepared the revolver even more carefully than usual. He loaded it so that the bullets would be fired in the order in which he had inserted them. He was careful to place the genuine bullet he had obtained so that it would be the last to be fired, at the Saturday performance.

The press had a field day when Alan Ackroyd was shot dead on stage on a Saturday in the play *Slaughter on Saturday.* 'You couldn't make it up', said Bert Atkins, reporting for the *Daily Mirror.* 'We don't usually do much reporting on plays, but this killing is too good to ignore', he said.

Bert went after the Detective Inspector who was investigating the murder. 'Who loaded the gun?' he asked. 'The props man', came the reply, 'but the chap who fired it says he always left the loaded weapon on a table in the wings after the props man handed it to him. He said was afraid of losing it. He said he was once in a panto where he had to throw a custard pie but lost it. He got into awful trouble.'

The DI sighed and added, 'These actors are a funny lot. Interviewing them is almost impossible. They never stop acting. They wanted to tell me who they thought had done it and why. I thought one chap was going to plead guilty for the publicity.' The DI shook his head then said, 'The props man who loaded the gun was the most sensible of the lot. He wondered if there might be some private grudge one of the cast or stage hands had against the dead man.'

John remained as ASM at the Maidstone Playhouse for thirty years. After touring companies became too expensive, a repertory company was formed to perform there, with the same actors being cast in a different play each week. From time to time, John was offered a small part. When they did *Twelfth Night*, he let it be known that he had played Malvolio and showed them his treasured press cutting. So it came about that he finally performed Shakespeare professionally. The local paper said his Malvolio made you fear for the revenge he might visit on anyone who upset him.

SCRUMPING

The flying bombs mentioned at the beginning of this story were pilotless monoplanes fuelled by petrol or a substitute. They were launched from ramps aimed at England from the coast of Europe. The engine of a flying bomb was located in a tube on top of the fuselage. The bomb was housed in the nose cone. When the fuel ran out, the aircraft would simply plunge to the ground and explode. The flying bomb was a random weapon of terror. It had to be attacked head-on so that the bomb in the nose was exploded in the air.

As the year 1944 unfolded, Hitler's war was beginning to draw to a close. Air raids were fewer, but final desperate attempts by Germany to subdue England with flying bombs and rockets launched from the other side of the English Channel were a threat. The communal air raid shelter in the local recreation ground was still in use in East Emsley, a London suburb, but the local boys preferred to stand on top and watch the Spitfires from Biggin

Hill taking on the flying bombs which, with typical tongue in cheek humour, everybody called Doodlebugs.

By 1944, Hitler's defeat was inevitable. Children evacuated during the blitz were back home and life had a semblance of normality. For seven young rascals who lived near to one another and went to the same primary school, the normal prankishness of boys was unsuppressed. One of their interests lay in stealing apples from an orchard attached to a house that had been bombed in the blitz.

'The old man's still living there', said Dicky Burke, 'so we will have to watch out.' 'No', said Johnny Evans, 'since the air raid the place is derelick.' But Dicky was the natural leader of the seven boys who made up the gang so stealing apples was the name of the game. The others wouldn't have been able to explain why Dicky led the gang, but he had authority.

'Well I ain't comin'', said Cliff, 'las' time he had a gun.' 'No he didn't. It was just a big stick', said Bob, who thought Cliff was a bit of a softie. Actually, Cliff didn't really fit in with the gang. His proper name was Clifton and his parents were regarded as a bit posh, especially by themselves. His mother didn't like him being called Cliff and would have been upset to hear him say 'ain't'.

Dicky said, 'We'll have to be careful if we're to scrump the old man's apples. Dave, you can be lookout. Blow that whistle you've got if you see him coming.' Dave readily agreed. He was very proud of the whistle given to him by his uncle Arthur last birthday. His dad, Arthur's brother, groaned when his son unwrapped it. 'Well', he said to his wife, 'at least it's not a blooming drum.'

Bert Wright, in his eighties and occupant of the war-damaged house with a fine orchard which was the target of the boys' plans, was expecting them back. Their scrumping added a frisson of excitement to his dull days as a widower. When a bomb had landed near his house, his high garden wall had been demolished so access to his property was easy.

The boys went home to dinner one day – Cliff called it lunch – after a morning's football in the park. They then rendezvoused at their base, a fallen tree truck outside the park, to go scrumping. Clambering over the remains of the broken wall round the old man's orchard, they headed for the apple trees.

Lookout Dave's attention was suddenly captured by something that was happening in the house. There was no sign of the old man but a number of men were moving about inside, carrying stuff. Dave crept round to the front of the house and saw a large vehicle into which men were loading the house's contents. Some of the old man's furniture and pictures and stuff looked expensive. Well, everybody knew old Bert was well off.

Dave made his way back to Dicky to report that the old man was moving so there was no need to worry about his coming out to chase them away. 'Moving?' said Dicky, 'That's funny. He told the local paper he was never going to leave the home he had shared with his wife for forty years. He was quoted as saying, "They'll carry me out of here in my coffin." He can't be moving.'

Dicky gathered the gang together. 'It looks as if the old man's house is being burgled. Let's forget the apples and see what they've done with him.' Carefully peering through a window into the kitchen, Chris, the youngest of the boys, saw the old man tied to a chair and gagged. Chris had never felt so excited. He felt like Dick Barton, Special Agent, whose weekly adventures on the radio were an important part of his life.

Chris excitedly reported his findings to the others who were crouched under the main window at the front of the house. Dicky took control. He gave Dave some coins and sent him off to phone the police. Then the remaining six crept round to the kitchen. It was deserted but for the old man. They ungagged him and he whispered, 'They're all upstairs. Get me out of here.' There was laughter in his eyes as he added, 'If you do, you can have all the apples you ever dreamed of.'

The police did not use a siren to warn of their coming so they caught the thieves in the act of emptying the upstairs of the house. There were three of them and, as they were marched off under arrest, one of them was heard to say, 'Bloody kids. We've been duffed up by a bunch of kids.'

The old man Bert was not in need of medical attention. In fact, he was full of beans and laughed as he said, 'You boys came to steal from my orchard but I don't think I'll tell the police. My hobby is cooking and it just so happens that I made a big chocolate layer cake yesterday. Would you like to eat it for me?'

While the boys sat round the kitchen table consuming the cake, Bert went off to the telephone. Shortly afterwards, the local press arrived to report the story of how seven boys had caught a bunch of burglars the police had been after for more than a year. Pictures of Bert with the boys featured on the front page of the local paper. Cliff had chocolate all over his face, which his mother said rather lowered the tone of the story and his place in it. So did his being identified as Cliff Rawlings rather than Clifton, she asserted.

A few years later the boys scattered to different schools for their secondary education. Two won places at the local grammar school after passing the eleven-plus, two got places at the local technical school and two went to the secondary modern school. All six flourished in different ways. Only one member of the gang failed to do so, namely Clifton Rawlings.

These were the days when parents could pay for places for their offspring at grammar schools if they failed the eleven-plus. Clifton's parents got him into the grammar school by this means but it was a disaster. He did not have the academic ability to cope with the demands of a grammar school education and descended into disruptive behaviour, bullying and rejection of authority.

Twenty-five years later, Clifton Rawlings appeared before His Honour Judge Richard Burke for attacking a policeman when arrested for shoplifting, a crime for which he had already spent time in prison following numerous offences of the same kind and others more serious. Rawlings was a sad sight after sleeping rough. He had no fixed address and no employment. Despite his appearance, the judge recognized his friend from scrumping days. He disbarred himself from hearing the case and arranged that Rawlings be brought to him in chambers for a private meeting separate from judicial proceedings.

Rawlings eyed the judge suspiciously after being ushered into his presence. 'Hullo Cliff.' said Dicky, 'Remember me? We used to go scrumping together.' The prisoner's mouth fell open with amazement. Then he began to cry.

His Honour arranged for Clifton Rawlings to be remanded into his custody as an alternative to a prison sentence. He then set about finding him a job and decent accommodation. With his life transformed, Rawlings abandoned his criminal ways and became just an ordinary citizen earning a living stacking shelves in a supermarket. A young woman social worker who had briefly been responsible for him in his bad old days met him by chance when they were both at a garden centre looking for spring plants. Their relationship flourished and the rest, as they say, is history.

Alison, for that was the woman's name, once asked Clifton, early in their new relationship, to explain what had happened to change his way of life. 'Well', he said, 'I met this bloke I had once been in a gang with.' Alison stopped him. 'Tell me no more', she said, 'I don't want to hear about the days when you were part of a gang.' 'We only pinched apples', Clifton protested. 'That', came the reply, 'started your life of crime. Many a lad has been led astray by scrumping.'

AFTERMATH

The year was 2100. The world had left one century and entered another. Boys in the sixth form at Ealing Grammar laughed with amazement when their economics teacher, John Nichols, started his lesson. He stated that, eighty years before, in 2020, everyone was walking about wearing masks because of a virus; all the shops and pubs and places of entertainment were closed; so were schools; everybody had to stay indoors; keeping yourself away from everybody else was essential.

The social consequences, explained the teacher, were disastrous, with many people suffering from depression. But even worse, in terms of the long-term effects, was the economic impact. John Nichols said, 'Think about that. What do you suppose were the economic consequences of what was called the lockdown?'

But before John Nicholls' carefully prepared exploration of the economics of the year 2020 and the years following could get under way, James Roper, lothario of the Lower Sixth, had a question that was nothing to do with the British economy. 'But sir', he asked, 'What about boys like us? How did they, you know, have a bit of fun with the girls if you had to keep away from one another?' 'Roper', replied the teacher, 'I might have guessed what you would be worried about.' A voice from the back said, 'Sir, Roper can't help it. He's a sex maniac. Ignore him. Let's do economics.'

'We know', said the teacher, 'what measures are available to a government when faced with an adverse balance of payments, don't we?' The class responded with the correct answers. The teacher went on to explore the much greater problems a government faced after borrowing multimillions to deal with collapsed businesses and widespread unemployment caused by the 2020 virus. 'The size of the National Debt was as great as it had been in 1945, at the end of the Second World War,' said John Nicholls.

He explained that, when a government needs to borrow for any reason, it does so by selling securities of different kinds on the stock market. If it wishes to borrow for a long time, it sells Treasury *bonds.* They are long-term fixed interest securities. The holder gets a fixed rate of interest each year in return for the loan. The government can terminate the debt by buying back the securities on the stock market. If a government wishes to enter into a short-term debt it sells Treasury *bills* which earn a lower rate of interest because the debt has to be settled sooner.

John Nichols said, 'When a government has had to borrow huge sums to pay for a war or, as in 2020, for the impact of a virus, it can end up with an enormous liability every year to pay the interest on the securities it has sold. It can have to pay such vast sums on the interest due to holders of the securities that it never has enough money to get round to buying them back.'

'Now', he said, 'can you think of anything in ordinary people's economic arrangements like that? Is there any way people borrow to spend?'

Jerry Blyth, the brightest of the embryonic economists in the class, got it right away. 'Sir', he said, 'credit cards. You can get up to your eyes in debt using one and not be able to do more than pay the minimum amount due on what you owe each month.' 'That's right', said the teacher, 'and it's been estimated that over fifty percent of people in this country are living way beyond their means by using credit cards as if they are money. They aren't. They are simply a way of spending when you haven't got any money.'

'Sir', said Jeremy Cook, son of a wealthy business man, 'my dad gave me a credit card on his bank account on my 17th birthday. He said I had to be careful in using it but thought I was old enough to be sensible. But he's taken it back. I went out

and bought a new top-of-the-range guitar with
it. When I brought it home, dad went spare.' The
sixth former laughed and added, 'My dad said I
was supposed to be studying economics but there
was no sign of it.' 'Well', said John Nicholls, 'you
have given us a perfect illustration of how some
governments go on.'

There followed a discussion of how members of
the class ran their personal finances. It emerged
that several of them carried credit cards. 'Be careful
when you get to uni,' said their teacher, 'there
will be great temptations to spend, spend, spend.'
'Especially on girls', said Roper cheerily. A voice
from the back offered the same message as before,
'Sir, he can't help it. He's a sex maniac.'

John Nicholls addressed the whole class in a
serious tone. 'There are economists who can't
handle their personal finances. Money is a good
servant so long as you keep control of it. Lose
control and disaster awaits.'

'Thank goodness,' he went on, 'that student loans
are a thing of the past. University teaching is back
to being free as once it was. There is no longer any
reason why you should graduate with a pile of debt.
Don't end up with a first in economics and your
finances in a shambles.' He smiled as he added,
'Better to get a second and be solvent.'

'We spent more than a decade after the virus
trying to reduce the National Debt. Crippling

debt was the pandemic's aftermath', declared the teacher. 'Don't let it be the aftermath of your going to study economics at university. And don't waste your abilities going to study any other subject. Economics is the secret to the future.' He paused, then added, 'Don't tell any of your other teachers I said that. The aftermath for me could be terrible. The classics department doesn't think economics is a proper subject.'

There was laughter as the class dispersed and someone called out as he passed through the classroom door, 'We'll come and visit you in prison, sir.'

A MAIDEN SPEECH

Stanley Brice MP was preparing his speech for the forthcoming debate in the House of Commons on the new bill on police powers. A newcomer to the House at 32, following a career in advertising, it was to be his maiden speech and he wanted to make an impact. He had been assured by the government Chief Whip, Jackson McLean, that the Speaker would call him early in the debate, as was the tradition when a maiden speech was to be made.

McLean was a man who never minced his words. He told the new MP, 'Make it good and one of the top brass may notice. You might be a parliamentary secretary before long. Mess it up and you'll sink without a trace and never be more than a backbencher.' He paused to give the advice he gave to all newcomers, 'Get to your feet, make your points briefly and succinctly, then sit down and shut up. Do not get into a debate with those around you. If you do, Mr Speaker will not be pleased and he is one whose displeasure you should avoid at all costs.'

Stanley, already quite nervous at the prospect of addressing what would undoubtedly be a full House, realized that his speech was even more important than he had thought. The new bill, increasing police powers, had already aroused strong feelings among MPs of all parties. It had also fired up activists of all kinds across the country. Should he have waited to make his maiden speech on some less dramatic occasion? It was too late for that now. The bill had already brought some fiery confrontations on the *Daily Politics* programme on BBC television, and on *Any Questions?* on the radio.

On one side of the exchanges were those who thought the bill did not go far enough; that the right to stop and search should be extended; that the penalty for resisting arrest should be increased; that anyone promoting violence during a demonstration or protest of any kind should be automatically imprisoned for a significant term; that the size of the police force should be doubled. Although the bill made little mention of sanctions, it had become clear that there were those who intended, during the bill's passage through the Commons and the Lords, to raise the issue of capital punishment for causing the death of a member of the police force.

On the other side, there were those who wanted to reduce the size and powers of the police force. Already, they insisted, the police were all too ready to resort to violence when attempting to carry out an arrest; that the policing of protest marches was carried out in such a way as to promote disorder;

that the police force was too often depicted in the media as accommodating racist bullies; that the provisions of the new bill would turn the country into a police state.

Stanley decided to begin his speech as dramatically and provocatively as possible. As he rose to begin his performance, there was an expectant hush in the House. Before his election, he had acquired a reputation for being a fiercely outspoken member of the Conservative Party. The press had written, 'This man does not know the meaning of moderation.' The Opposition were looking forward to baiting this opiniated newcomer to the government back benches. They were about to learn that he was equally keen to bait them.

'Mr Speaker', Stanley began, 'let me begin by reminding honourable members, and the several dishonourable ones over there' – he pointed towards the Opposition benches – 'of what Trotsky said ...' He got no further. There was uproar. The Speaker called for order and intervened. He looked extremely displeased. So did Jackson Mclean. He was furious that the new MP had so blatantly disregarded his advice not to upset the Speaker.

'Mr Brice', the Speaker said, 'please do not bring that kind of language here. If you abuse Her Majesty's Opposition, you will not be called to speak again.' Sir Henry Blackstone, for he it was who occupied the Speaker's chair, paused and, as was his custom on occasions, introduced a little humour to the proceedings. 'Let me make it clear', he said, 'that you are only allowed to insult your opponents politely. You will learn how to do that by observing the behaviour of those who have sat in this House a long time.' There was laughter and old hands nodded their heads knowingly.

Stanley Brice was humbled but not discouraged. 'My apologies', he said, 'I guess I was following the example of that mighty parliamentarian Nye Bevan who once declared that all Tories were vermin.' 'Yes', said the Speaker, 'but he said that outside this House. You can't say that kind of thing here. Please continue, but use a little moderation in your vocabulary.' He emphasized the word moderation.

Bill Cobden, a Labour member who would be Father of the House if he got re-elected next time, said to the woman beside him on the Opposition benches, 'This Tory clown won't last. His seat is marginal. We'll beat him next time if we put up a chimpanzee with a stutter.'

Stanley Brice continued his maiden speech. 'Trotsky believed in what he called a state of permanent revolution. He said a first step in achieving that was to discredit and destroy the police force. Only then could capitalism be brought down.' He paused and added, 'Mr Speaker, at this time in the history of our nation, there are forces at work to undermine the authority of the police who guard and protect us and to make policing our streets impossible. We are threatened', he loudly declared, 'with nothing less than anarchy.' The benches behind him cheered, those opposite howled in protest.

The new MP moved on to his second point. He said, 'Centuries ago at Runnymede, the rule of law became the basis of our way of life. Magna Carta says: *Nullus liber homo capiatur nisi per legem terre.* That 39th Article of the Great Charter means our freedom depends upon the *legem terre,* the law of the land.'

'For God's sake', said Bill Cobden, 'who does this piece of Tory vermin think he is, coming here and spouting Latin at us?' But the Secretary of State for Education looked delighted and said to those around him, 'It's a long time since we had a Latin lesson here. There's hope for the classics yet.' A voice behind him said, 'It's a long time since we had Magna Carta quoted at us too.' Another voice said, 'It's time someone reminded us about the Trots.'

Stanley Brice spelled out his message: 'The role of the police is to enforce the law and so defend our freedom. Without a strong police force, our freedom will evaporate. At our peril do we fail to strengthen and support the police. Anyone who does not support the new bill, which has that purpose, will be letting down those who elected them to serve here, and will give heart to the anarchists who want to destroy our democratic institutions.'

The newcomer drew to a conclusion 'Mr Speaker', he said, 'you have rightly advised me to practice moderation in my use of language in this House. I accept that guidance. But surely moderation should have no place in our response to those who would destroy our way of life.'

Stanley sat down to a resounding acclamation from the government side. 'This man has a future here', said the Home Secretary, who was the driving force behind the new policing bill. Clifford Bax, the shadow Home Secretary, known as Bax the Butcher for his ruthless demolition of opponents, declared, 'We'll have to sink our fangs into this young upstart at the first opportunity.' In the press gallery, the man from the *Guardian* was pleased with his piece which he had headed, Tories Back a Police State. It began: 'There will be police on every corner when the new bill passes. They'll arrest you for dropping a fag end.'

'Well done on your maiden speech' said Jackson McLean to Stanley Brice, 'it began badly but came good, although I thought you were pushing you luck with the Speaker at the end. I think you'll survive in the jungle', he said, 'but watch out for animals looking for prey.'

Four years later, Stanley was number two in education as Minister of State with responsibility for schools. His brief was to review the curriculum. He had hopes of making Latin a required option for examination classes. He put his favourite quotation from the Magna Carta on his desk at the Ministry. It reminded him of his maiden speech in the House of Commons.

A SCHOOL STORY

Jack Simmons, who taught history at Blairgrove, an independent grammar school for boys in London, strode into his class of fourteen-year-olds and declaimed, 'All things are possible to those who believe!' He surveyed the thirty boys in front of him. 'Who said that', he asked.

Several hands went up. Winston Churchill had a number of supporters, so had Martin Luther, who had been the subject of a recent lesson on the Reformation. 'Sir', said John Bickerstaffe, keen supporter of West Ham United, 'Billy Bonds said it when the Hammers were drawn against Arsenal in the FA Cup.' The class laughed, especially the Arsenal supporters among them.

'Bickerstaffe', responded the teacher, 'we all know that your interest in history doesn't stretch far beyond your team's record, but the history examiners are unlikely to give you any marks for knowing the Hammers story of triumphs and disaster.' 'Sir', said a voice from the back, 'mostly disasters.' More laughter.

Jack Simmons liked to get the class laughing. But they all knew better than to go too far. The teacher's fury with anyone who seriously misbehaved was fearful to behold, although some of the more perceptive boys realized that Simmy was a bit of an actor.

'I'm still waiting for the right answer to my question', the teacher insisted. 'All things are possible to those who believe. Who said it?' A confident hand went up from a boy at the front. 'Sir', he said, 'Jesus said it to the man who brought his epileptic son for healing and asked Jesus if he could help.' 'Oh gawd', muttered Bickerstaffe, sniffing contemptuously. His parents had no time for religion and their attitude had been passed on to their son.

'You are right Hendry', said the teacher, 'Well done. Tell us more.' 'Well', said Graham Hendry, whose dad was a Methodist preacher, 'the man brought his son to Jesus and said please help my son if you can. Jesus replied, If? All things are possible to those who believe. And the father came back with, I believe. Help my unbelief. The story means a little bit of belief is enough for a start in anything.'

'Thank you, Hendry', said Jack Simmons, 'you are a very brilliant young man, with a very attractive personality.' There were groans all round. The teacher's extravagant praise of any boy who got a question right was a running joke. He surveyed the class. As their form teacher, he knew each of them well. 'I know what some of you are thinking', he said, 'this isn't an RE lesson so why are we getting Jesus stuff. It's because what Jesus said is very much to do with your public examination prospects next school year.'

The boys were alert. 'Look', they were told, 'you will only pass if you believe you can. But Mr Stone, your physics teacher, tells me a few of you have given up and aren't bothering. Yes, I know the coefficient of linear expansion isn't everyone's idea of fun, but there's no reason why you can't get to grips with it if you put your mind to it.' He paused, then drove home his message, 'You can all pass in every subject. You wouldn't be at this school otherwise. So I don't want to hear any more complaints about you in the staff room.' Some of the class were surprised to discover that Simmy had even heard of the coefficient of linear expansion. 'I thought he only knew history', said one. 'I think he knows us a bit too well', responded another.

The staff room was full of interesting characters. The school had first been established in the eighteenth century during the Enlightenment. The younger teachers thought some of the old guard looked and talked as if they had been appointed at the opening in 1743. The school's character was extremely traditional, not least because a third of the staff had been pupils and, after university, had returned to teach at Blairgrove. New ideas advanced by young men recently appointed were treated with smiling indulgence, then ignored.

The appointment of a new, forward-looking Headmaster, James Luscombe, had not pleased the Vice Master, who saw himself as guardian of the school's traditions. Luscombe's fate was quickly sealed at morning break one day.

Richard Oxley, head of classics – let no one presume to call him Dick – was a stalwart of the old order, which included certain responsibilities taken up without formal recognition. One of Oxley's duties that he had assumed during his thirty years at the school was to preside over the completion of *The Times* cryptic crossword during morning break. Others gathered round to assist.

Having resolved to get the staff to be more punctilious in getting to their classes, the new Headmaster swept into the staff room as the bell sounded for the end of break. 'Gentlemen', he declared, 'the bell has gone for lessons.' No previous holder of the Headmastership had ventured into the staff room. It just wasn't done.

The crowd around Richard Oxley parted, like the Red Sea as Moses led his people across. Turning in his seat to address the intruder, he who lived in a world of Latin declensions said imperiously, 'Headmaster, we haven't yet completed *The Times* crossword.' The intruder sensed an atmosphere of great hostility. 'Oh, I see', he said and made a tactical retreat, his authority destroyed. 'What a blundering fool', said Lionel Glenfield, head of geography and the most outspoken of the old brigade. Within a year, James Luscombe had departed.

Jack Simmons, in his third year of teaching history at the school, was sorry to see Luscombe go but realized that his attempt to dislodge the influence of the old guard had lacked sufficient subtlety. He kept his thoughts to himself but realized that things would have to change in view of the direction in which the education system was going. He would, he reflected, love to sort out the school but was sorry he would never get the opportunity.

Simmons' appointment as an assistant master for history had raised a few eyebrows among the Oxbridge caucus on the staff. He was a graduate of the London School of Economics, the LSE, an institution of London University with a reputation for radical politics after being under the influence of Harold Laski for some years. 'Good God', said Lionel Glenfield, on hearing of his appointment, 'he's probably a Marxist.' He turned to the head of classics and said, 'You need to watch our Oxley. Latin will have to give way to RS, Revolutionary Studies.'

The new teacher's studies at the LSE had embraced a wide range of subjects in addition to economics, most notably history, which Blairgrove had appointed him to teach. At his interview, he had tentatively indicated his readiness to introduce economics to the curriculum, as many top schools were doing.

The Chairman of Governors, an old boy of the school who had grown wealthy in the world of commerce, welcomed the idea. 'School recruitment is becoming increasingly competitive', he told his fellow governors, 'We need to keep ahead of the game. Aske's now has an economics sixth form. We should have one.'

When a new Headmaster was appointed to replace the one whose outrageous intrusion into the staff room had been such a disaster, Jack Simmons gave him time to settle down, then went to him to suggest adding economics to the curriculum. The new man, Roger Clough, said, 'I was going to see you about that. The Chairman of Governors mentioned it at my interview. But', he said, with an amused expression on his face, 'let's not rush in and upset the mighty defenders of the school's ancient traditions.'

He said more. 'The trouble is, we will have to find the salary to appoint someone to cover your history teaching. Our budget is tight. I don't think the Chairman thought of that. I'll discuss it with him.' He smiled and added, 'I think he wants us to produce some economists who will become rich bankers and business men who will give much gold to the school.'

Within three years, economics had become an option for those boys choosing their examination subjects. Outstanding results among sixteen-year-olds led to a steady increase in numbers studying economics at A Level. It demolished the school's classical tradition. 'I did warn you', said Glenfield to Oxley, who decided to retire.

The head of classic was not the only grumpy one. There was unease in the staffroom when it became known that Blairgrove could no longer afford to continue its independent status. It struggled for a while as a voluntary aided school, which brought some financial support from the local authority, but the tide of education politics was, slowly but surely, floating the Blairgrove ship into the harbor of local authority control. 'Just you wait and see', said Glenfield, 'they'll turn this place into a comprehensive.' Not for the first time, his opinion proved prophetic. 'It's teaching geography you see', he said, 'it means you know which way the wind is blowing and in what sort of country you will end up.' Some of his hearers weren't sure about the analogy but didn't risk arguing with Glenfield when he was pontificating.

Roger Clough had no desire to remain at the school in its new comprehensive status and, being a keen yachtsman, gave way to his yearning to go down to the sea again. He invested his lump sum on departure from the headship, plus his savings, in a new boat which he named *Blairgrove Departure*.

The question of once again finding a new Headmaster for Blairgrove exercised the minds of the new governing body of the school. It was heavily weighted with local authority representatives, but a few of those who had known the school in its previous manifestations remained. The most notable of these was Grace Beckwith.

How her arrival as a governor in the school's independent grammar school days had come about was down to Major Beckwith, a long time member of the governing body. It so happened that his wife Grace, a civil servant and leading figure in the Department of Education, brought their daughter, a university student, to school prizegiving at Blairgrove. At home afterwards she was asked by her father what she thought. Being an outspoken young woman with modern opinions, she said, 'Looking at the governors on the platform, they looked a right bunch of male chauvinists. You need a woman or two.'

At the next meeting of governors, the Major expressed the view that it might be helpful to have a woman appointed to join them. 'Mind you', he said 'it would have to be someone who understands our way of doing things. We don't want a suffragette sort of female.' He laughed nervously. Sir Henry Dace said, 'Good idea. A woman's point of view would be valuable. After all, all these boys have mothers.'

Nobody was sure what Sir Henry meant by this. It sounded to the Major like a *non sequitor*. Others thought the same but challenging Sir Henry was something one avoided. He was a philosophy academic at UCL and could argue for England. 'What about your wife?', inquired the Chairman, 'Mrs Beckwith knows the school and knows what the politicians are up to in education.'

Little did the governors know what they were letting themselves in for when Grace Beckwith agreed to become one of them. 'But darling', said her husband, 'give yourself time before you reveal your formidable side.' In the matter of a Headmaster for Blairgrove Comprehensive, Grace asserted, 'The answer is under our noses. He is already on the staff.'

She went on, 'We have a man here who started his career at Blairgrove when it was a highly selective school; he has been largely responsible for reconstructing the curriculum and bringing it up to date; even in the old days he always showed as much interest in boys who found learning difficult as he did in the wiz kids. When he was offered the post of Vice Master, he accepted on condition that it be changed to Deputy Head.

'I recall', said Grace Beckwith with a smile, 'the time when he proposed the change of title. He said that Vice Master made it sound as if the holder was in charge of dealing with the sexual adventures of the older boys. Didn't we laugh! But then, Mr Simmons has a great sense of humour. That's one reason he will make a great Headmaster.' Which, in due course, he did.

KNOWING WHERE
YOU ARE COMING FROM

At a seminary for the training of Church of England priests, the Reverend Jeremy Upton, who liked to be called Father Jay, was appointed to the staff in 1995. An academic historian before ordination, whose special subject, on which he had written several books, was the Reformation of the sixteenth century, he was a controversial figure.

As a member of the history department at Keble College, Oxford, he was regarded as something of a reactionary, committed to narrative history rather than the more fashionable thematic approach. What irked some of the younger tutors was his inclination to challenge the teaching of history by themes. 'That way', he would assert, 'you can end up knowing everything about a subject but have no idea about the sequence of events. But history is all about sequence. That's what the very word history means.'

Father Jay arrived at the seminary at a time when modernization had changed, and was continuing to change, the liturgy of worship. His arrival was a response to the Principal's alarm that many young men and women coming forward for training had only slight knowledge and understanding of the origins of the Church of England. Along with that, many appeared ignorant of the Book of Common Prayer, to which some elderly worshippers, and some not yet elderly, were deeply attached.

When the novelist P D James, a leading figure in the Prayer Book Society, came to the local cathedral to address a public meeting, students at the seminary were encouraged to attend and listen to her *apologia* for the preservation of the Book of Common Prayer. One student was heard to say afterwards, 'I never thought of any of that.' The incident persuaded the Principal of the seminary to appoint Father Jay.

He soon stirred things up by joking about what was known as fresh expressions of worship. He protested that turning worship into a cross between a pop concert and a fun day at Butlin's might increase a congregation but did nothing for folk who wanted some good old-fashioned Bible preaching. He said, 'I guess it's no bad thing that many of today's churches have developed two quite separate congregations – early morning churchgoers who love the Book of Common Prayer and the gingangoolie generation who don't want anything too heavy.' One of the seminary tutors who thought otherwise said, 'Worship should be fun. The days of long sermons grinding out tales of ancient kings and prophets with unpronounceable names are over.'

Father Jay's popularity with students owed a lot to his personality. His ten-word opening salvo was much imitated by students. 'Now mark this', he would say to each new cohort, using a pompous pulpit voice, 'you must not take religion too seriously.' He would pause then go on, 'People used to take religion ever so seriously when the C of E was started. As a result thousands were tortured on the rack for believing the wrong things. Crowds would turn out to see them disembowelled or burned at the stake or decapitated. Now that', Father Jay would insist, 'was not the kind of spectacle to go and watch on a Saturday afternoon just because Man United weren't playing at home.'

'But,' he went on, 'that gruesome record is part of our Anglican heritage; a permanent reminder of horrors that can arise from disputes about religious belief. It's important that you should know where the Church of England is coming from. That must never be forgotten. The sequence of events in history is critical, and helps us understand where we ought to be going. Lose the first piece of a jigsaw and you will never be able to grasp the whole picture.'

After covering the history of Henry VIII's battles with the Pope, who eventually issued a bull calling on Henry's subjects to overthrow him, Father Jay devoted his series of lectures to the Book of Common Prayer, the bedrock of the Reformation. His treatment of it was a combination of respect and hilarity.

For the most part, explained Father Jay, the Book of Common Prayer was the work of Thomas Cranmer. He was appointed Archbishop of Canterbury by Henry, being the driving force behind the king's claim to be supreme head of the new Church of England and no longer subject to the authority of the Pope. Cranmer's greatest achievement was his authorship of the original Anglican liturgy as set out in the glorious language of the Book of Common Prayer. 'Its literary impact is still enormous', insisted Father Jay, thumping the lectern in front of him in the lecture theatre, 'as is its spiritual power for many Anglicans. Remember that when you have care of their souls.'

In his exploration of the book, Father Jay would start with the section headed *Prayers and Thanksgivings*, and focus on this prayer:

O God, the Creator and Preserver of all mankind, we humbly beseech thee for all sort and conditions of men; that thou wouldest be pleased to make thy ways known unto them, thy saving health unto all nations.

'That beautifully constructed sentence', claimed Father Jay, 'embraces several fundamentals of the Christian faith of enormous importance today. Firstly, it asserts the creative power of God; secondly, it recognizes his continuing involvement in human affairs; thirdly, it assumes his commitment to people of all kinds.'

'Don't be put off', suggested Father Jay, 'by the sentence not being gender free. As they used to say before the politically correct brigade got to work, man embraces woman. Not only does the term "all sorts and conditions of men" include women, it may also be taken to include the growing multiplicity of sexual identities developing today.'

A hand went up. 'Father', said the student responsible, 'are you suggesting that Cranmer was aware of what was going to happen in the field of sexuality?' 'Well', came the reply, 'as the Bible says, there is nothing new under the sun. If you look at what men and women got up to in Tudor England, today's try-anything-you-like society would not have surprised them. No, I don't think Cranmer was being consciously prophetic, but his words do have an echo in today's world, do they not?'

The second half of the sentence in question next received Father Jay's attention. He pointed out that the plea for God to make his ways known to all nations raises a question of huge importance in a multi-racial society where different faiths prevail.

He asked, 'What makes Christians think they have got the right idea about God and everybody else will tumble to it sooner or later?'

The rest of the lecture was taken over by a discussion of that issue. A young man who had converted from Islam to become a Christian was a particularly stimulating contributor. He said, 'The social and ethical teachings of Islam are very close to those of Jesus. My Christian perception of God the Father is not light years away from how I used to think of Allah. Perhaps all religions are travelling on different roads towards the ultimate truth about our Creator. We should be talking to one another, not lobbing grenades from our particular trench at those in another one. The crusades of the Middle Ages must have broken God's heart, and Allah's. Are we not', the young man asked, 'as one Eastern mystic has said, just walking each other home?'

The response to that was clamorous and Father Jay chose not to interfere. He sat down behind his lectern, smiling as exchanges became heated. A student of evangelical tendencies pointed out that, before engaging with other faiths, the church needed to sort out its own divisions. A young woman of liberal views responded by insisting that, for a start, evangelical Christians should stop attacking those who didn't share their views. 'They used to say', she asserted, 'that the Church of England was the Conservative Party at prayer. Well, today it ain't.

I'm a member of the Labour Party, so there!' The clamour increased with groups of two or three in the lecture theatre having vociferous debates among themselves.

One of a group of trainees for priesthood from the Ivory Coast of Africa said, 'If the liberals take over the church, there will be schism – and I'll be leading it. Missionaries from England came to Africa to teach us the way of Jesus. Perhaps it's time for us to be sending missionaries to England.'

'Well', said Father Jay, smiling, 'it's good that so early in this course it has become clear there are deep divisions among you. It should help you to understand the England of Henry VIII and his offspring, and the Book of Common Prayer.'

He went on to relate some Tudor history. He described how, in July 1536, Henry devised and published what became known as his Ten Articles, setting out for the first time the doctrine of the new Church of England. In a letter to his bishops, Henry explained the purpose of the Articles:

> They were devised to establish Christian quietness and unity among us, and to avoid contentious opinions. Of late, to our great regret, we are credibly advertised of diversity in opinions as have grown and sprung in this realm such as to cause danger to souls and outward inquietness.

'I suppose', said Father Jay, 'that having invented a new church, Henry had to tell its members what to believe. But is the Church of England in this day and age not still locked in the same debate?

'Mind you', he went on, 'we don't apply the same punishments as Henry did on those whose personal theology is different from our own. We just shout at them across the room, as some of you did just now.' He heard one student say to another, 'Five centuries, and not much has changed, has it?' He picked up on this and said, 'We sometimes think things have changed dramatically in the modern world but on occasions we deceive ourselves. The patriarchal nation over which Henry VIII reigned is not yet completely gone from English society. You will have to cope with that in your priestly ministries, especially you women. Knowing where the Church of England is coming from may help you understand that and cope with it. Never forget the narrative of church history.'

Some weeks later, as Father Jay's series of lectures on the Book of Common Prayer drew to a close, he having covered the whole gamut of issues thrown up by Thomas Cranmer's work, he smilingly expressed the hope that students had been disturbed by the series.

'Look', he said, 'you will come across Anglicans who are still deeply wedded to the Book of Common Prayer, often because they grew up with it and have beautiful passages from its liturgy, which they know by heart, as a support and stay in their lives. Such folk need your tender loving care as much as those who are in the vanguard of change.'

Father Jay drew his teaching to a close declaring 'May God help you to survive in the maelstrom of church politics. May your churches not be stretched on the rack of disputation and may none whose care is your responsibility lose their heads. God bless you all and amen.'

PURSUED

There is a poem about the divine love that pursues us in our lives as we search restlessly for love and contentment. *The Hound of Heaven,* written in 1890 by Francis Thompson (1859–1907), depicts God's determination to overpower us with his love if we will submit to Him. The poem begins:

> *I fled Him, down the nights and down the days*
> *I fled Him, down the arches of the years.*

Thompson struggled all his life with opium addiction, which was a sort of flight from reality in his search for meaning in his life. He at first had an ambition to become a priest and his sense of a divine presence never left him. One writer has said of the poem *The Hound of Heaven* that it describes the author's flight from and recapture by God. His flight was fuelled by the fear that he would have to give up other, less savoury aspects of his life:

> *Though I knew His love who followed*
> > *Yet was I sore adread*
> *Lest, having Him, I must have naught beside.*

So comes the climax as God the pursuer declares:

Rise, clasp my hand and come!
Ah, fondest, blindest, weakest,
I am He whom thou seekest.

An almost exact contemporary of Francis Thompson was George Matheson (1842–1906), author of a hymn that bears traces of *The Hound of Heaven*. It echoes my personal Christian pilgrimage which began with my being at first affected by, then influenced by, eventually overpowered by a sense of the presence of Jesus Christ in my life.

Amazingly, the hymn has survived without any updating of words or meanings – a sometimes unhappy device of modernists. Each authorized version of Methodism's hymn book published in the twentieth century, namely the 1933 *Methodist Hymn Book* and the 1983 *Hymns & Psalms*, left George Matheson's masterpiece just as he wrote it. The same applies to the latest authorized version published in 2011, *Singing the Faith*. It is a hymnal rock upon which one's faith may be founded:

O love that wilt not let me go,
I rest my weary soul in thee;
I give thee back the life I owe,
That in thine ocean depths its flow
May richer, fuller be.

There is no other way to explain the passage of my life than that it has been driven by divine guidance, intervention and empowerment. Early Methodism's emphasis on personal salvation – God's offer of a personal relationship with the individual – is no longer fashionable. Its revival, without abandonment of commitment to social improvement, would do wonders for a church in which many yearn for greater closeness to God in their personal lives.

The reality of God's closeness is realized for me in my relationship with Jesus. That may be a stumbling block for some. They are at ease with the vague notion of God who is in some way behind creation, but they struggle with the person of Jesus Christ as someone who was God's embodiment in human form and *who is still around in spiritual form to befriend us.*

Been there. Done that. My own pilgrimage took me through the dark valley long ago where my faith was not anchored in a relationship with Jesus but in the belief that God is a good chap who wants us all to be good and thereby to change the world. That is barren territory. But once we place our faith in Jesus, he will see us through the dark valley.

So how do we get to know him and discover his friendship and power? Let me recommend three steps. Firstly, we need, regularly and repeatedly, to read Mark's account of the Jesus story. It is based on what the disciple Peter told Mark, the author. It is the first account of the Jesus story to be written and is the shortest and most spellbinding account. Secondly, we need to commit ourselves to getting close to Jesus, who promised he would come again and does so in the Holy Spirit. Thirdly, we need to believe in letting him take control and be prepared for what happens as a result. One of the most important things he ever said was, 'All things are possible to those who believe.' So, be warned, this is dangerous stuff.

Asking Jesus to take control will make things happen you may not have intended. I have had occasion to say to him when his Spirit does its stuff: 'Here's another fine mess you have got me into. I hope you know what you're doing.' He always does, and he has made my life wonderful. Not free of worry, of course. But one's anxieties become less and less as the blessed assurance that Jesus is in control increases, with the knowledge that all will be well.

Keep in mind that the guidance Jesus gives comes to us in a variety of ways: through things we read; through what someone says to us; through some words in a play at the theatre or on television; at a service of worship; in an incident that makes us think. The secret of getting to know what Jesus may be saying to us is to be constantly alert and expectant. There's no dozing off in the Christian life. The commitment is total. I know that Jesus, the hound of heaven, will never let me go.

THE DYING
OF THE LIGHT

Jack Dacre was a man who enjoyed disputation. In his career as a leading figure in motor manufacturing, he had often been called upon to address staff conferences set up by other firms. He could be depended upon to wind up his hearers. 'Get Dacre', said the chief executive of a struggling textile firm, 'we don't want our staff spending the day half asleep or playing on their mobiles. Giving them an away day is not for them to relax and enjoy themselves. We want to get something out of it.'

A friend of Dacre's who had heard him address a number of different groups once said to him, 'Why do all your speeches sound like the Battle of the Somme?' 'Because', came the reply, 'the business world is a battlefield. A firm will only survive and prosper if everyone on the staff is committed to its objectives. The same is true of any institution.'

The way in which Dacre opened up at a manufacturing conference set the tone. His usual strategy was to loudly declaim:

Good morning. Is it? Am I supposed to say I'm glad to be here. Well, I'm not. When my staff see that my car isn't in the car park, those newly appointed will think they can relax. But they'll learn pdq that they can't. Leadership, you know, means persuading people to get on with the job because they are part of a team working for survival and success. There's no such thing as a free lunch and there's no such thing as a free day. Did you think you were having one? Well, you're not. If you don't use this day well, you'll get sacked tomorrow.

'Are we meant to take this chap seriously?', said Harry Blake to the chap seated beside him. 'I'm not taking any chances', came the reply, 'so let's shut up and listen.'

Having got his audience thoroughly roused, Dacre changed to a more conversational tone. 'Look'. he said, 'thirty-eight percent of the firms in the British economy are only just making enough to keep their shareholders happy and all their staff on the payroll.' He paused and smiled. 'No', he said, 'your firm is not one of those.' There were sighs of relief in the room. 'But don't bank on it staying that way if you don't pull your weight. The world of business is a battlefield and and we are all down there in the manufacturing mud.'

David Yeoman, a leading figure in the management of the firm running the conference, was a keen student of history, having read the subject at Trinity College, Oxford. Dacre's words brought to mind Max Hastings' book 'Catastrophe' about the battles in the mud in Flanders during the First World War. He turned to the colleague beside him and said, 'This man know how to alarm you, doesn't he?'

During the rest of the day, the three hundred staff of Albright's Agricultural Equipment Limited attended sessions in small groups, each of which had to do with some aspect of the firm's work. The leader of each group had been carefully selected by the firm's management as being capable of getting people talking about possible improvement. The hidden agenda given to each group leader was improving commitment to the firm's future. Jack Dacre went from group to group and stirred things up if they seemed too passive.

The conference was held at Stamford in Lincolnshire. About ten miles away was the famous Oakham School, where George Albright had received his education. He invited his old headmaster to attend the conference and stay for lunch with him and the main speaker. The headmaster had been impressed with Dacre's opening salvo about staff working together for survival and success. He thought about having an inset day and invited Dacre to speak. It became the first of several invitations from educational institutions. Jack's wife, an opera buff, told him, 'Once you've organized the business world and the educational world, how about moving on to classical music. The management is a shambles.'

A heart attack brought Jack Dacre's speaking career to an end. But his liking for aggressive disputation did not diminish in old age. He kept on his desk at home Dylan Thomas's words:

Do not go gentle into that good night,
Old age should rave at close of day;
Rage, rage against the dying of the light.

He raged about just about everything. The state of the world appalled him. The government was run by ninnies; the economy was mishandled; the media were in the hands of scoundrels; what passed for entertainment was a disgrace; the behaviour of the young was out of control; climate change meant the planet was doomed; even a cup of tea didn't taste like it used to.

Sadly, Jack Dacre's greatest rage became focused on his grown-up children. His son Benjamin had become a social worker; his daughter Julia a midwife. He complained to his wife, 'Neither of them is making any money. What have I worked so hard for so that we have plenty of it?' His wife suggested he talk to them about it, knowing what they would say and hoping it would make him think again about his attitude, which was driving her up the wall.

'Come off it, dad', said Ben, 'what has all your money done for you? You're just a grumpy old man fed up with everything. You can't buy your way out of that.' Julia had a more gentle personality. 'Look dad', she said, 'Ben and me are both working to make life better for people. I help mothers to bring people into the world as easily as possible and he helps those who have problems to handle them. You ought to be proud to have helped create us. We are working to make planet Earth a better place.' Ben added, 'Stop grumbling, dad. You heart should be singing. Me and Julia are very happy.'

In bed that night, sipping his hot chocolate, Jack said, 'Those kids of ours are wonderful. You know, they have a lovely attitude to life.' 'Yes' responded Evelyn, his relieved wife, 'I know. They're great.' She hesitated. 'And just you wait until you get to know Julia's intended.' 'What?' said Jack, almost, but not quite, grumpily, 'Nobody told me our daughter had an intended.'

'She's only just sprung it on me', came the reply, 'but she's twenty-six you know. His name's Martin Swinburne. They've been going out together since last year, but I didn't think you'd noticed. I've told Julia to bring him to dinner on Saturday, when I guess he'll ask you for your permission to wed our little girl. Isn't it exciting?' 'Well', said Jack, 'I'll want to know if he's earning enough to support a wife'. He paused and added, 'and family.' Evelyn laughed. 'He's a paediatric consultant at the Royal,' she said, 'not bad at 32. Well qualified to be a dad, as our Julia is to be a mum.'

Over dinner, Martin revealed that his father was a local councillor, which turned the conversation to politics. Ben held his breath, fearing that his father would embark on his rant at politicians. He need not have worried. Martin said, 'Actually, my father is pretty scathing about local politicians, and even more so about the government. He says that when you get to know and work with politicians, you realize what ninnies some of them are.' Jack thought to himself that he liked this man. In the old days, he could have done business with him. The dying of the light wasn't so bad after all.

PARTING MESSAGE

Alison slipped her hand out of Joe's to retrieve her handkerchief. Like many of the women in the cinema, there were tears in her eyes. They were watching the film 'Gone With the Wind', originally made in 1939 and now, more than thirty years later, the subject of brilliant technical updating in its colour, sound and special effects. When first shown, the film had won no fewer than three Academy Awards, for best film, best actress and best supporting actress.

Vivien Leigh, an English actress, had been cast in the female lead as Scarlett O'Hara, after over a thousand hopefuls had been auditioned, including most of the biggest American stars. But arguably the most dramatic of the Academy Awards, for best supporting actress, went to Hattie McDaniel, who played Mammy, Scarlett's black woman servant. Such was the important relationship between Scarlett and Mammy, which was depicted as one of happy dependence, that some critics felt the film offered an apologia for slavery.

As 'Gone With the Wind' reached its heart-breaking climax, sobbing could be heard in the auditorium around Alison and Joe. Rhett Butler, played by Clark Gable, had just told the beautiful, flirtatious, capricious Scarlett, who had too often yearned for another man, that he was leaving. Desperate, she replied, 'If you go, what shall I do?' His reply became the greatest exit line for a wronged man in cinema history: 'My dear, I don't give a damn.' Among the sobs in the cinema, there were a few quiet cheers from men.

Alison and Joe were regular cinemagoers. When their relationship had gone beyond mere friendship, they had one Saturday gone to the pictures to see Ralph Richardson in 'Home at Seven'. It was a tale of a London suburban businessman who lost a day of his life to amnesia, as a result of which he was suspected of a crime.

Walking home holding hands after that, Alison suddenly announced, 'I want none of that coming home late from the office when we're married.' 'Hey', replied Joe, 'I haven't proposed yet'. 'But you were planning to, weren't you? I could tell.' Not for the first time, Joe realized how sensitive and perceptive was the girl with whom he had fallen in love.

During a romantic exchange on their second wedding anniversary, Alison said, 'I fell in love with you when we were both in the sixth form', 'Really?' responded Joe, 'I rather fancied you in your school uniform. I dreamed of being your school tie, hanging round your pretty neck. But I was very shy in those days. A lot of us boys were scared of you girls.' 'And a good thing too, cheeky lot', the girl replied, then thoughtfully added, 'But I guess you were cheeky because you weren't sure how to handle us. Teenage boys are very insecure.' Joe thought she was probably right, but didn't say so.

That night, in bed, Alison said, 'I think you should know that you will have a teenager to handle not all that many years from now. Doctor Fraser says so.' Joe laughed. 'I was waiting for you to let me know you were pregnant. We boys can tell.'

Nineteen years later, with twin girls, Joe and Alison rejoiced in their clever, conformist daughter Hannah and lay in bed worrying about her sister Jane who gave every sign of wanting to start a revolution. Jane announced at dinner one day that she intended to take part in a forthcoming demonstration against climate change caused by capitalist exploitation of workers. Her father furrowed his brow and asked her how she worked that out. 'Just think', she said, with irritation in her voice, 'of all those workers years ago working for next to nothing in factories spewing black smoke into the atmosphere so the bosses could make a fortune. Those fortunes have been inherited. We ought to confiscate them.'

'It's no good arguing with her', said Alison. Having surreptitiously joined the Socialist Workers Party, Jane steadily became more eloquent in promoting her radical agenda for the world. Cleaning her room, her mother came across pamphlets and booklets arguing the case for revolution. When she told Joe, he said, 'You shouldn't be cleaning her room. She should do it herself.' 'But she won't', said Alison, 'she says she likes it in a mess.'

Things came to a head when Jane appeared one morning in torn jeans, boots and an oversized T shirt. She wore a quite heavy chain round her neck like a necklace with a large metal disc hanging from it that said: BREAK THE CHAINS OF CAPITALISM. Hannah, home from university, loved her sister and admired her courage. She said, 'Well, you can't say she's half-hearted about it, can you?'

Joe decided he had had enough. 'Look, Jane', he told her, 'we can't go on like this. The neighbours think we are mad to have you in the house. When we tell them you are our daughter Jane they say; "Never. That's not the Jane we knew."' 'OK', the girl responded, 'it's time for me to leave. I'll pack my bags and get out of your life.' 'But what will you do?' said Alison. 'Well, for a start, I might hitch-hike to Moscow', she laughingly replied.

Jane suddenly became serious. 'Look', she said, 'I have plenty of friends who think like me. I will go and join them in a place they have. And I will still be earning from my writing.' Jane was a qualified journalist with an NUJ union card. Her articles on events in the news regularly appeared in left-of-centre newspapers and journals. 'That's all very well', said Joe, 'But what about us? We will worry about you.' Jane delivered an unanswerable response: 'Father, I don't give a damn.'

Jane made her way to the commune established in an empty property in Belgravia. The police did not move the occupants on, preferring to know where they were in case of trouble. Jane was welcomed warmly by her friends. 'Hey, Janey, you've got a bag. Does it mean you're staying?' 'You bet', replied Jane, 'I've just delivered the greatest exit line in the history of an escape from parents.'